*This collection takes its name from a series of experiments by the psychologist Harry Harlow. He set up baby rhesus monkeys with two mother-shaped objects: one made of wire, and one covered in soft cloth, either with a feeding bottle potentially attached. The monkeys preferred the cloth mother, even when it provided no sustenance.*

Published in the United States and Canada by Whisk(e)y Tit: www.whiskeytit.com. If you wish to use or reproduce all or part of this book for any means, please let the author and publisher know. You're pretty much required to, legally.

ISBN 978-1-952600-44-9



Cover design by Bri Chapman

# Wire Mothers

## Katharine Goldiron

Whiskey Tit
VT/NYC

*For everyone who lived with a wire mother –
including, possibly, Harry Harlow himself*

# Contents

# The First Snow

This was the night before the first snow. The cousins were visiting from down South, and they'd all piled into the house. Multiple cousins. Indistinguishable cousins. Just a mass of youth. Mother bedded them on any horizontal space she could find with blankets from the basement (laundered especially last weekend), sometimes only wads of socks stuffed in spare cases for pillows. Cacophony had ruled for hours on end that Saturday, and evening, descending, felt alien. No: magical. No: holy. One of these three but not the others.

Bodies wound like clocksprings, barely twitching eyelids. Jill was the only one up, looking at their faces, this or that feature betraying kinship. Her father's jaw, her mother's short upper lip. The weird fuzzy hair that appeared in one of four siblings per generation. (Not a family stingy with siblings.) The light to study their faces came from the moon, early and blinding. The cousins had flawless skin and fine brushed eyebrows. Jill's own arm, in that light, was freckled and sprouting with dark hair, like a boy's. Mother told her this would pass. She'd been embarrassed about her own arm hair at fourteen but it had thinned and blonded out with time. Jill nevertheless considered sloughing it off with a razor, though this seemed too odd to mention to Mother, either as request or decision.

At school, on Friday, Hunter had asked her to come. He'd asked her to bundle up and meet him at midnight Saturday. It was his birthday Sunday morning, and he understood they couldn't be together because of the cousins, but he asked her to stay up late and when the moon was bright, to come across the lane and across the cleared land where Mr. Zavodnik kept his beehives (beeboxes, really) and across the little copse where that boy had gotten lost when she was a very little girl. Hunter asked her to meet him at the edge of the woods by his daddy's place and give him a kiss as a birthday present. His first birthday present for his fourteenth year. Right after midnight. It would be romantic, he said.

She sat up in a twin bed which cradled two other bodies (Tetrised together, lengths and widths balanced inside the narrow rectangle) and peered out the window. No snow yet. Just the impalpable sound of its approach, the muffled middle C of an orchestra tuning. The tension of the sky, clouds massing.

*

The older boys told Donald that the best place to kiss a girl for the first time was someplace high up. The highest place Donald knew was the bell tower at his church, which had a black iron spiral staircase that shrieked worryingly, metal-on-metal, above and below you but not under the step on which you stood. Donald had been courting Patti Kellerman in every possible way for two full weeks now, and she had laughed at his jokes and accepted his sweaty palm against her cool dry one, accepted his arm draped across her shoulders with all the casualness of a wire spooled away from a stick of dynamite, while they sat in his mother's car at the drive-in with his sister Meredith chomping popcorn in the backseat, the paired stench of salt and butter turning his stomach, Patti's soft cool dress brushing his chest as she turned to snag a few kernels and chat to Meredith (she was a grade above them at school and thus possibly more interesting to Patti than he, Donald, the boy with his arm across the pink cardigan thrown over her very shoulders, was), and when the man in the movie kissed the woman in the movie, and then the monster jumped out of the shadows and knocked her down and threw her over its shoulder and carried her off, he shifted just slightly and came away with Patti's sweater stuck to his arm, the fabric's heat derived from his skin and not hers. She went on chattering to Meredith with bare shoulders. Her body, inside its dress, pressed back against him as she turned further around in the seat, as if he were a part of the car, a bony cushion with explosives embedded in the upholstery. The cardigan fell and squashed between them.

So he imagined that asking Patti to go up to the bell tower with him might push things along. He invited her to church with his family for the following Sunday and she cooed with delight. "Your family sounds *divine*," she said. *Divine* was big just then—malteds, new 45s, nominally handsome teachers all sheltered under its umbrella. She took his arm and squeezed it like a nurse checking his blood pressure. Her high, flowery perfume addled his senses.

*

Earlier in the afternoon, one of Jill's uncles had set rabbit traps in the yard. Mother had been trying to grow a vegetable garden throughout the fall, but rabbits had devoured every zucchini bud, every lettuce leaf. "What's the point now?" she asked, leaning against the railing on the back steps. "Frost's come and gone."

"It'll show 'em," said the uncle, and snipped off a bit of wire smartly with red-handled cutters. The trap had a noose of wire meant to close around the rabbit's unlucky foot, biting into it, holding the animal there until its captor woke in the morning and ambled out after coffee to turn it loose.

"It'll show 'em. Teach 'em all a lesson."

"I don't think rabbits learn like that," said Mother.

"All animals learn from pain, Meredith," said the uncle.

"That's nonsense," said an aunt, distracted from refereeing a game of Red Rover nearby. The family dog, a barrel-chested Rottweiler mix named Michael Jackson, kept trying to play along, such that much of the aunt's work consisted of keeping him from knocking anyone over. "In experiments, those mice keep pressing the button over and over. They never learn."

"That doesn't even make *sense*," said the aunt's teenage daughter, draped langorous over a plastic chaise. "You're not even talking about *pain*. That experiment was about *orgasms*."

"Heyyy, Hilary," said Jill's father, tilting his head toward the Red Rovering cousins in earshot.

"Anyway animals can *too* learn from pain," said Hilary.

"And these rabbits are going to," said the uncle. "Mitch, put in another stake over there."

"It just seems a little late, Don," said Mother. "After the frost."

"Never too late to close the barn door," said Father, laughing. Mother shrugged and went in the kitchen and came out with a bowl of carrot and potato peelings, which she emptied into the incinerator across the yard. Hilary wore sunglasses, but she pushed them up on her forehead so no one would miss it when she rolled her eyes at Father's quip.

She was sleeping (or listening to her Walkman, or filing her nails, or whatever) by herself up in the attic. She'd insisted. Icicles presumably hung from her pert little nose by now.

Jill eeled out of bed around its two other occupants and crept into the living room. Children reclined in orderly ranks on the carpet, like mini-soldiers in a makeshift ward. She tiptoed around their hands and feet and heads. The uncle sleeping on the couch had gone elsewhere, and Jill cuddled under his blanket. It wasn't time yet. She meant to leave at ten of twelve, and it was only 11:20.

Hunter had been patient with her. She was timid. No one had ever even felt her up. It was probably her churchy family, her discomfort in locker rooms, the hard German consonants in her last name. Other girls knew the sinews of boy-bodies, knew their heft and their scarce soft places. Hunter's body was a strong sapling in JC Penney's clothes. She wanted to spread her hand on his chest and see if his skin was warm. The ferocity of this image, rising like a soda-bubble before she went to sleep, her hand atop his skin, over his beating heart, frightened her. Especially because Hunter said that he cared about the Jill inside her head and heart, not the Jill inside her clothes. Of course she thought that was nice of him, but she cared about the Hunter inside his clothes. She longed to know if, out of them, he was as ordinary, as inconsequential, as she was, or if he was something different altogether.

She gazed out the picture window. The moon was now totally obscured. No scudding puffs, but a thick woolen duvet, lighter than gray, nearly the vague watery white of Grandmother's tea set. Yes. Snow. The front had rolled south across Lake Erie and here it was now, the loveliest silence of all, waiting for the conductor to stride out and take a bow and begin.

"Jill?" It was Tina, from the floor. "Is it snowing?"

"Not yet."

"Can I stay up and watch?" She extracted herself from her sleeping bag (actually Jill's sister's sleeping bag, green with a disfiguring paisley rash) and crawled under the uncle's abandoned blanket. "I've never seen snow before."

"Me neither." Jerome, from his own sleeping bag.

"Shut up, dork," said Tina. "Go to sleep."

"Make me."

"You've never seen snow at all?" said Jill.

"It's too hot for snow in Biloxi," said Tina. "Is snow heavy when it lands on you?"

Jill began to say no, but Jerome said that was a stupid question, and they bickered in whispers until the rest of the cousins had popped their heads up, like prairie dogs, to watch the fun.

"It's not heavy by itself," Jill cut in, "but it's heavy in a shovel or on top of a car. The wetter it is, it's heavier."

"Does it come wet or dry?"

"It can't be dry, dummy. It melts, like ice."

"You've never seen it either. I'm asking Jill."

"She could tell you if you'd shut your cake-hole."

And so on. Kids. Jill lost the thread when a clump of cousins from Mobile started up about a broken window for which one of them had been punished severely and unjustly, when really it was Ratface Ben down the street who broke it and ran off, and Ratface's mom lied like a dog when she said he was at a piano lesson, because everyone generally agreed that Ratface couldn't play a piano if he had four grubby hands instead of two. Another clump of cousins resumed a heated dialogue that had been going on for years, apparently, about whether Obi-Wan was a better Jedi than Luke, and Tina and Jerome got going because Jerome hit Tina on the arm and claimed that it didn't hurt, while Tina argued that it did. In the middle of all this, getting louder and veering toward physical injury, the uncle walked in with the neck of a kicking rabbit closed in his fist.

It began to snow.

*

Patti came to church in a sweet little hat and white gloves, like an older or richer girl. (The only hats in Donald's church were worn by the wives and daughters of Mr. McDougall, who owned the paper mill.) Donald's chest glowed at the sight of her walking toward the church steps, so pretty and well-pressed. Something about her stride, her carriage, spoke of confidence borrowed and donned, like her mother's coat, with only her uncertain body beneath. Unbutton the coat, and you unbutton the girl: or so Donald hoped, thinking of the bell tower. The glow moved southward.

The plan was for Patti to sneak away to the bell tower immediately after the service ended. Since this was not her church, no one would notice her, or say anything. Donald would linger and make conversation for a little while, and then he would follow her. He didn't have an answer when she asked why the secrecy, or what was so important that he wanted to show her up in the tower. But she agreed.

She did not take the hat off during the sermon. Donald could only see Meredith's dishwater blond ponytail on the other side of the hat (polka-dotted, with a tiny, useless net veil). Usually he watched Meredith's nose with peripheral vision and nudged her when it started to dip. Father Bowers droned like a table saw and Meredith rarely slept well: a recipe for napping in church, to their father's ire.

Today her ponytail trembled as Father Bowers declaimed on the foolishness of coveting thy neighbor's anything. Donald had never seen her so cheerful on a Sunday morning. She even helped with breakfast, refused coffee. Their father rewarded her with a kiss on the nose.

When the organ set upon them, go in peace, Donald whispered "See you soon" to Patti and meandered with his parents into the cloud of relieved chatter. It sounded like savages' native tongues. Patti's cool dry hand; the crisp wave in her hair. Her lipstick. Maybe smeared.

Ten minutes later, the staircase groaned. A hiss and giggle floated down the shaft and settled on Donald like snow. Human sounds. He lifted his feet, one and then the other, to the next and the next stair, trying not to shift or shatter the rust that bound the staircase to its girders, its bolts. More reached him—underhum of vocal cord, whisper of cotton. Yes, someone was up there with Patti. Who could it be? She knew he was coming, didn't she? She wasn't with another boy, was she? *All I want is a kiss,* he told the staircase, to shut it up. *I'm not asking for much.*

Shadows moved against the wall. Silhouettes. He climbed. One of the shadows had a sweet little hat, one a ponytail. Donald twisted, near the top, the floorboards at eye level, saw what Patti and his sister were doing, and light struck his retinas from all angles, rendering him some species of snowblind.

*

"None of you should be awake," said the uncle. The rabbit emitted weak noises. "What the heck are you doing?"

"I'm sorry, Daddy."

"Jill, did you wake everyone up?"

"No, Uncle Don."

"We wanted to see the snow, Daddy."

"They were curious," said Jill.

"All children are curious," said the uncle. The rabbit kicked air. "They also need their rest. I don't want a bunch of sleepyheads tomorrow morning."

"Let's go back to bed," said Jill. She stood and spread the uncle's blanket back across the sofa. "C'mon, everybody."

"It's snowing!" cried Jerome and pointed out the window. No one looked, except the rabbit, who might have been looking. Tina crawled into Jill's sister's sleeping bag and the rest of the prairie dogs settled back into their ranks.

The uncle caught Jill's arm. His hand bled freely from a gash across the root of his thumb, and the immediate stain on her nightgown appeared black in the snowlight. "You get back up to bed," he said. "I don't want to hear anything about this tomorrow."

"Yes, sir," said Jill. She went upstairs. The other two cousins in her bed were nowhere near awake, but she stood by the bedstead for a moment, looking out the window at the snow falling thicker, quieter still. She ran her fingers over the hair on her arms.

It was 11:40. *I must get dressed. I can't let Uncle Don—*

The kitchen door closed with a thump beneath her. She looked down at the yard. The uncle carried the rabbit out the back door. From above, Jill could see a shiny spot at the back of his head. The snow formed a kind of glitter on his hair.

On the picnic table lay a pair of kitchen shears, Mother's yellow dish gloves, and a black garbage bag. The uncle muttered something that Jill could just hear, but could not comprehend, over the deafening silence of the snow, the sleeping house. Mother's gloves went on one at a time, while he passed the rabbit back and forth.

Then he picked up the kitchen shears and snipped through the fur at the back of the rabbit's neck. The animal kicked wildly. Holding it by the head, he yanked at the bloody opening until he stripped the fur off. The rabbit still lived. It pulsed. It bled. He placed the pelt, almost in one piece, on the black garbage bag and broke the rabbit's neck with a swift twist. The uncle whistled (it came faintly through the glass) and Michael Jackson trotted up to the picnic table. He sniffed the rabbit, glanced at the uncle, and set to. The uncle removed the yellow gloves and patted Michael Jackson's head. Then he tossed the rabbit skin into the garden, among his traps, to be buried by the snow.

Jill sat on the floor, holding the rungs of her bedstead, not yet nauseated. *What animal deserves to be skinned alive?*, she wondered, and I wonder that too.

*

No one saw Patti fall. *I can't imagine who'd do such a thing*, they said, and/or *she had so much to live for*. But no one wanted to ask the kids who were up there with her what happened. Do you blame them? Meredith didn't speak a word for several weeks, and Donald started going for walks after dinner, walks so long and cold that he'd find himself two towns over at dawn with freezing snot on his sleeve. He finally kissed a girl named Bobette, whom none of the other boys wanted to dance with, at a cotillion at the church basement that fall. Everyone looked who'd looked away when the ambulance came for Patti.

*

The cousins thought they'd dreamed about the uncle in the middle of the night with a rabbit. No one mentioned it. There were snowballs to make, angels to form, before it all melted in the warm afternoon. Mother had found the rabbit skin in the garden, and thrown it into the incinerator with any number of other secrets, by the time someone found Jill, blue and still and perfect, half a mile from the house.

🐵

# Between Four and Six

Every afternoon between 4 and 6, I get so hungry I cannot sit still. Nothing I eat satisfies me, not toast or cheese or peanut butter or fruit or an entire bag of microwaved popcorn.

My boyfriend asked me to stop buying chips and crackers at Trader Joe's. We don't live together, but he visits a lot. He told me snacks always disappeared before he had a chance to try them, so I ought to stop wasting money on them.

"I just get so hungry," I told him.

"Can't you do something else?" he asked. "Distract yourself?"

"I can try," I said.

The next day, at 3:45, I opened a book, a Georgette Heyer novel. She always absorbed me, her plots as fluffy as meringue, a confection to dive into tongue-first.

I noticed the hunger at 4:19. I looked at the clock, and back at the page. My stomach settled its claws into my cerebellum.

Heyer described high tea at a country house: scones with cream and jam, cucumber sandwiches, cubes of white sugar melting in hot dark tea. I salivated. The characters nattered about love and intrigue. *Get back to the scones*, I urged them.

In turning a page, I tore a corner of it off. Unthinking fingers brought the paper to my mouth. The creature inside me leaped at the scrap.

I stared down at the page, and then deliberately tore a long strip down the center. Fed it between my lips like spaghetti. It nourished. Tore the rest of the page off and slurped it down. My stomach curled up on itself and dozed until suppertime.

The next day, I didn't wait. As soon as 4:00 came, I ripped another page of Heyer's prose away from its spine, tore it into bite-sized pieces, and fed myself. The creature was hungrier that day, so I ate nearly ten pages before I'd satisfied her.

My boyfriend's daughter (he's separated, not yet divorced) came for dinner that night. He brings her over often, so she can get used to me before we move in together. Feeding a toddler occupied so much of my attention that I hardly touched my own food, but that was all right. I felt full and yet light, as if I could live on air.

For days I ate my Heyer novel, and when it was gone, I started another one. My appetite kept increasing: thirty pages a day, fifty. I gobbled them fearlessly. She wrote dozens of novels; I was not consuming the irreplaceable.

"You seem different," my boyfriend said. "Have you lost weight?"

"Yes," I said. I had. But I also felt different: cooler, more relaxed. And I kept saying odd things. Or saying normal things oddly. "Do keep playing, dearest."

He lifted the saxophone again. "Whatever you say, Duchess." A string of resonant notes plumped out of the bell, so juicy I wanted to snatch them out of the air and swallow them whole. Why not? I could eat anything.

The next book was *Wise Blood*, which took me only a week to consume. At a party that weekend, I said clever, violent things and listened at the edges of people's words, where their desires lay. My hostess raised her eyebrows at me and sipped her wine. "Have a heart," my boyfriend whispered under the music. I thought of God, and death, and laughed.

The following week I ate *Orlando*. I chopped my hair off and stopped shaving my legs. My boyfriend's daughter cried when she saw me, but so light and fresh was I that only a kiss on her chubby cheek set her giggling. My hunger ripened, and I ate *Maus*, growing morose and thoughtful, heavy with dye and history. I twitched invisible whiskers at noises.

I went faster, swallowed more and more: short books like appetizers, long books like casseroles. *Try me*, shelves whispered. *I'm nutritious and lean. Try me, I'm full of meat and sex. Try me, I'm the answer to your hunger. Serve me with a cream sauce and gnaw on my heart.* Bookstores made me lightheaded; the scent of all that food, crisp and dusted, tempted me beyond lust.

My own stores dwindled. A book a day went into my throat, and no private collection could keep pace with such hunger. Still, I saved money on groceries, as mealtimes came and went without arousing my appetite at all. I was only hungry at teatime.

"Something's going on," said my boyfriend. "What's gotten into you?"

"Books," I said.

"You've always been a reader," he said. "That's not what I mean. Your personality changes every day, it seems like. Are you on some meds I don't know about? Or off them?"

"No," I said. His daughter banged on the table with a spoon and I held her little fist in mine. She shoved her other hand in her mouth and chewed. I fully understood. "It's my new diet, I guess. It's changing things up."

"Look," he said, "you're freaking me out. Will you do me a favor?"

"If I can."

"Will you lay off the diet for a week? Just to see if you feel any better?"

"I feel terrific," I said. "Yeees, peaaaars, mmmmm."

"Do it for me," he said. "As an experiment. Just one week."

Why not?

On Monday I was all right, except that I was hungry for dinner for the first time in months. I ate a cheeseburger and felt better, but not satisfied.

On Tuesday I couldn't stop looking at the remaining books on my shelves (browned paperbacks with C-shaped spines, picked up for fifty cents apiece at the library: dried beans, in another woman's pantry), so I went for a walk. The uncovered windows of houses sometimes revealed books inside, left on end tables, or sleeping upright with their sisters. I stared at them, let my mouth fall ajar. Then I shook myself and walked on.

On Wednesday I prowled, desperate. I drank hot tea. I ate salami straight out of its vacuum pouch. I chewed ice. My stomach roared and plunged.

On Thursday I tore a page from the sheet music my boyfriend had left on a stand in my living room. I chewed it into a sticky wad and swallowed it. It wasn't the same, but my head cleared. Soon, Bach replaced the song of craving that pounded through my skull. But it didn't last.

On Friday night, my boyfriend came for the weekend with his daughter. I stalked out of the bedroom when I heard him come in. He dropped his overnight bag with a thump. "My God," he said.

I looked at the child in his arms. So clean, so plump. She wasn't quite what I wanted, but she might do. My appetite granted me a single moment of disbelief, and then I pounced.

# *To-Do*

- ~~Rent van~~
- ~~Pack~~
- ~~Go grocery shopping~~ (HEALTHY snacks)
- ~~Buy new Kidz Bop CDs~~
- ~~Write letter to M., deliver~~
- ~~Pick up, 2:30~~
- Get to Hampton Inn in Chicopee (make reservation?)
- Enjoy the kids!!

The euphoria wore off a surprisingly short time after she herded them into the van, and then the Kidz Bop CD dissolved into an unintelligible backdrop of noise, and she became aware of a cool black sphere of panic behind her left ear. Lily had no idea what to do, then. Her certainty sank and dissolved like sugar in iced tea.

Her mistake was in not giving herself enough items to cross out on her to-do list after picking up the kids. Enjoying them didn't seem enough to fill up the time, the black void, and anyway she'd forgotten how their presence could grate and grate until her nerves bled.

"Gran Lily!"

"What!" she shouted. "I'm sorry, Bren. Gramma was thinking. What is it?"

"Where are we going?" Brenna shrilled. "We never take the highway home."

"I told you already," she said. "I told you at school. Rory, can you remember what I said?"

"Going on a trip," he answered promptly. "An adventure."

"Righty-o." Lily returned her attention to the road.

"But where?"

"Someplace special."

"Is Mommy coming?"

Last night, in her little house in Palmer, twenty miles and an impassable distance from her daughter's in Southbridge, Lily discovered an apparent "spirit animal" inside herself. An idea she'd dismissed as hippie hooey. But there she was: the lioness. It was ten months to the day since Melanie had bellowed *Get out or I'll throw you out*; long enough for Lily to finally comprehend that it could be a year, two years, forever, before she saw her grandchildren again. And *poof*, the lioness made herself known. She stamped and roared around the little house: *I should just take them away. I should just take them away and raise them myself. Better than I raised you.* Now, at the mention of Mommy, the lioness growled, low and soft.

"She's not coming yet, Brenna-bun. This is a special adventure, just you and Rory and Gran."

"Whyyyyyy?"

"Because I say so." She turned up the music, which was a prepubescent chorus rendering "We Are Never Ever Getting Back Together" in bright, horrific pastels.

"I hate this," said Rory. "Is there any other music?"

"I can't change it while I'm driving," Lily snapped, and then smiled at him in the rearview. "Sorry, buddy."

"What's the *matter* with you, Gran Lily?" That was Brenna again. "You're acting so *mean*."

Lily had no memory of her being such an ill-behaved pest. Melanie had been a snippy little thing through a certain phase, but it passed long before she was Brenna's age. "I'm sorry, honey," she said a third time. "I'm just trying to get us there safe. Okay? Just trying to watch the road."

In the absence of something next on the to-do list, in this in-between place, Lily could not seem to organize her thoughts. The black sphere thrummed *what have I done, what have I done* while the lioness yawned her approval and the rest of her brain shucked and jived about whether she'd fastened Rory into his booster seat properly and whether they had enough juice boxes back there. And about when exactly Melanie had outgrown being rude.

Well, maybe she hadn't outgrown it at all. Maybe the current version of Melanie, the one who was as permissive as a defrocked priest about what her children consumed, allowing them to read books much too old for them (Brenna had a book with the word "murder" in the title; only eight years old and reading about *murders*!) and eat food that was all sodium and sugar (frozen macaroni and cheese, Costco cookies; even their apples were apparently pre-sliced at the grocery store)—maybe this Melanie was merely the sassmouth four-year-old Melanie stuck with a bicycle pump and inflated to adult proportions. It was from under the nose of that four-year-old, Lily told herself, that she had snatched Rory and Brenna. From that irresponsible child.

Snatched. *Baby-snatcher*. A new word imprinted in neon against the cool blackness. Hardly babies, though, these two. Brenna eight, Rory already five. They were old enough to make up their own minds, to leap happily into Gran Lily's arms when she came to pick them up at school. Since their mother was late (again). They hopped in the van willingly.

Not babies. Not snatched.

• Get to the Hampton Inn in Chicopee

She'd chosen Chicopee because it was crummy, cheap, a place Melanie wouldn't think to look for her (*I can go slumming too*, the lioness snarled). The kind of town that [w]itch Connie could have called home. And she'd picked the Hampton Inn because it was a trustworthy name, likely an okay place to take a couple of kids.

The traffic on the Masspike was to be expected, but after twenty minutes of stops and starts, Rory moaned. "I'm sick, Gran Lily. I'm gonna—*ooohh…*"

Nowhere to pull over. She glanced around inside the van. A plastic Walmart bag jammed with animal crackers, mini Yahtzee! and magnetic checkers games, and more wretched Kidz Bop sat on the passenger seat. Lily upended it and its contents went everywhere; she passed it back to Rory just in time for him to unload the bright orange cheez-n-crackers he'd had for an afternoon snack into it.

"Eeeww," said Brenna.

"Is it leaking?" said Lily.

"No. But it *stinks*. Can I open the window, Gran?"

Lily powered down the front passenger window, and Masspike Stew flooded in—exhaust, hot pavement, cigarette smoke, a hint of the trees in flower to the right of the breakdown lane. "Hang in there, honey," she said to the rearview. "We're almost there."

"Almost *where?*" insisted Brenna.

To

• Get to the Hampton Inn in Chicopee

she could now add

- Stop at a drugstore:
    - Ginger ale
    - Pepto (just in case)

It was a relief to put something else on the list. As long as there was something to do, the gibbering thoughts that floated out of the black sphere didn't bang around quite so loudly inside her skull. She took the exit ramp gently, trying not to jar Rory around too much.

"Help me look for a drugstore, Brenna?"

"No."

*No?* "It's for your brother, honey. For his tum-tum."

"His *stomach*," said Brenna with infinite disdain. "I won't do nothing till you say where we're going."

"Won't do *anything*," said Lily.

"Won't do *nothing*."

She'd forgotten how they could infuriate you, could wear your mind down to a soggy lollipop stick. "Look for a CVS. Even a gas station...*there*." She put on her signal and eased the big van into the parking lot of a Walgreens. "Wait here just a minute, all right?"

There was a hassle at the checkout. A young man at the counter couldn't decide on a flavor of chewing tobacco, customers stacking up behind him, and when a second clerk finally opened a second register, the soft-bellied stoop-shouldered gray-faced man behind Lily cut in front of her. The nerve.

"I have children in the car," she fumed at the clerk.

"Six eighty-three," he answered.

Just outside the store, she halted hard. A young fellow stood at the open passenger window of the van, hanging his elbows inside. He wore khakis, gleaming brown belt and shoes, a crisp blue button-down. "What kind of games do *you* like to play?" he asked into the van as Lily stepped off the curb.

She could hardly breathe, but it still had to be handled just right. *What are you doing to my children*, she rehearsed. Yes, that was good. With a note of hysteria to unbalance him. "What are you doing to my children?"

He looked at her across the hood. "Oh, hi, there." He offered a faltering little wave. "I'm waiting for you, I guess. These're your kids?"

"Get out of here, you *creep*!" Her lips tingled with righteousness.

He took a half-step closer to the curb, his jaw tightening. "Look, lady. I wasn't…you left them here with the engine running." He directed his words away from the passenger window. "Anyone could have come and driven off with 'em. I just kept an eye out till you got back."

He wasn't following the script. The kettle boiling inside her gave off a whistling scream. "How dare you. You *creep*. I only left them for a minute. And you just swoop down like God's own—"

"It was seven minutes, by my watch," he cut in. "A little longer and I would've called the cops."

Lily's knees went weak at this thought, but the lioness was awake now, her tail thrashing. "Get out of here," she said, stalking halfway around the hood of the van. "I'll call the cops myself. You're *harassing* me. You're harassing my *children*."

The man raised his hands and backed off a few steps. "Take it easy," he said. "I'm going." Glancing around the parking lot, he jogged to a black Altima and escaped, his tires squealing over the painted lines of his parking space. He was going too fast to have jotted down her license plate.

Once in the van, "Drink that," she said, and thrust the can of Canada Dry at Rory.

"I don't want it."

"It'll settle your stomach, honey. Just drink it."

"I feel fine," said Rory. "Can I have some animal crackers?"

"That was a nice man," said Brenna. "He asked us about our five favorite things. Mine were all Star Wars."

"That's great, Bren." Lily crooked her neck to look through the back window, past the children. The engine leapt, but the van went nowhere. She'd shifted into neutral instead of reverse.

As they wended through Chicopee, Brenna fell quiet, whether from sullenness or introspection or something else, and Rory's carsickness cleared up commendably. Although he started singing "I'm Henry the Eighth I Am" in a murmuring sort of way over the execrable Kidz Bop CD, a purchase Lily regretted more than nearly any other in her life, aside from the lingerie she bought in 1994 that made Gordon laugh at her when she modeled it for him, and Rory just would not let up, singing softly but persistently, "I got married to the widow next door...she's been married seven —*times* before..."

The parking lot at the Hampton Inn was sparsely populated. The sun kept hiding behind clouds and bursting out again. "We're here," said Lily, her foot on the brake, her hand gulping for a shifter that wasn't there. Oh, right, up by the steering wheel.

"We're *where?*" cried Brenna, zero to distraught in two words. "*Where is Mommy?*"

"You'll see her soon. We're on an adventure, Brenna-bun."

"Don't call me that," spat Brenna. "I hate you."

Lily shut off the ignition and slammed the door hard enough to make the van rock on its wheels. She hoped someone *did* drive off with 'em this time.

- Check in
- Get the kids settled

Half an hour later, Rory and Brenna lying on their tum-tums and captivated by SpongeBob cavorting on the TV, Lily stared at the polymerized wipe-clean wallpaper and racked her brain for what to put next on the list. She'd done what she set out to do. She'd gotten the kids out of that toxic house. Like evacuating them from a room full of poison gas. That Connie, her radical haircut and her furious eyes. Melanie and her eternal maternal failings. Like being raised by wolves! They're better off here with me, with me here. I know what they need.

Shoot, I left the rest of the animal crackers in the car. Where should I take them for dinner? McDonald's. Melanie loved McDonald's. All kids do, don't they?

"I wanna go swimming," said Brenna. "There's a pool here."

"You don't have a bathing suit," said Rory.

"I can swim in my underwear. Remember sometimes *Mommy*" (this word was directed at Lily with venom) "takes us to the pool by surprise on Fridays? We do that then."

"That's our pool," said Rory. His hands were tightly balled against each other, his feet pushed together. "Anybody might be at this pool."

"I wanna go swimming," Brenna said again.

"We can go if you want to," said Lily. "C'mon, Rory, it'll be fun."

Rory looked like a little old man witnessing Beatlemania, his mouth withered in disapproval. "It's *not* our *pool*."

"Our pool isn't our pool either. It's the neighborhood's pool." Brenna hopped off the bed and pattered to the bathroom to retrieve a towel, its nap worn thin with bleach. She mimicked Lily's voice unkindly. "C'mon, Rory, it'll be fun."

- Take the kids swimming at the pool

The elevator kept stopping at in-between floors and opening on nobody. It smelled like a diaper pail, the bright false note of disinfectant atop human stench.

A surprising number of people were enjoying the indoor pool, which was large and heated and roofed at the shallow end with dim, curving panels of glass, like the old smoking sections at Shoney's. Late-afternoon sun filtered through, dancing on wet skin. Large red letters painted on the wall shouted NO LIFEGUARD ON DUTY and SWIM AT YOUR OWN RISK!

Rory, wary at first of stripping down to his Batman underoos, was soon shrieking and splashing with the other nomad kids. Brenna was only just young enough to get away with swimming in her polka-dot day-of-the-week panties, but Lily didn't spot any creeps by the pool (or any nosy parkers like Mr. Seven-Minutes-By-My-Watch). Just a few over-padded moms and colorless, flabby dads. And one Aryan-type couple with 2.3 perfect blond children.

Lily, thinking about the kids getting dehydrated from the chlorine and the wet heat, went to the lobby to see about a few bottles of water. The front desk clerk sent her to the hotel's little restaurant, where a bar was open. Warm wood, leather stools, flatscreens posted here and there burbling early-evening programming.

After paying through the nose for three water bottles, she decided the kids were fine where they were—all those puffy parents to watch out for them—and sat at the bar. One glass of wine, just to settle her nerves. Rory and Brenna wouldn't miss her, surely. They were having fun.

The cool black sphere was much smaller, now, following the distraction of coping with actual children for a few hours. It was hard, harder than she remembered, but she clung to her certainty. There was no one else who could do this. Melanie was too preposterous to mother them. What kind of person "comes out" after ten years of marriage and two children? And takes up with a...a...*biker chick* from Boston (probably Bar Harbor, in reality)? And cuts her only loving mother out of her life? She didn't disapprove of lesbians, oh no, nothing like that, but Melanie was obviously *mistaken*, she was such a fool for boys in high school, giggling on the phone to her girlfriends all night long. This was just another phase. Anyway, Lily had been through dark times, too, weeks when she couldn't stand another moment of Gordon's nasty comments over breakfast and cruel hands after bedtime, and she stuck it out until their family was finished, like a woman should. But Melanie couldn't, not even with a man as fine as Ryan around. No. She had to *be herself*. What kind of person gives in to such foolishness, turns everybody else's lives upside down because of some *fad*? No kind of mother. No kind of daughter.

"Excuse me." A nice-looking gentleman around her age, smiling. "May I sit down? I won't bite."

"Of course." Lily shifted the water bottles one by one to her left. She fought the urge to pat at her hair. "I'd love some company."

"That suits me. I never do get used to sitting at a bar alone."

They chatted. His name was Randolph—not Randy— and his wife had passed away prematurely eighteen months earlier. An embolism. They had gone everywhere together, even when he was on business, as he, a consultant, frequently was. Now he traveled alone and rarely found anyone pleasant to talk to.

Her face warmed. She lied and told him she was a widow, too. Plenty of time to correct this wee fib if things progressed the right way. Single, handsome, travel-happy men didn't sit by her just every day. She sipped her wine and tittered at his jokes.

Randolph's attention flickered to one of the TVs over the bar. He tsked and shook his head. "I hate these," he said. "So many children missing their mothers."

The local news was on. The white words on their restless red background dashed against her like a bucket of ice water.

## AMBER ALERT
## 2011 GRAY DODGE GRAND CARAVAN,
## MA 9CD-R30
## FEMALE, AGE EIGHT / MALE, AGE
## FIVE
## TRAVELING WITH CAUCASIAN
## WOMAN, EARLY 60s, 5'6", 160 LBS
## STATEWIDE

I am not 160 pounds, she thought. I'm 140 if I weigh an ounce. She began to formulate something to say in response to Randolph, something about mothers and children, but one of the flabby dads from the pool rushed in. His face was almost as pale as his Hanes t-shirt, and he was barefoot.

"Yours is the little boy in the Batman shorts?"

Her heart knocked in her throat. "What is it?"

"He's unconscious, swallowed some water—"

She flew down the burgundy-carpeted hallway, burst through the glass doors. The pool was turbulent but empty, the echoing tile walls near-silent, everyone standing in a little huddle of varying heights near the NO LIFEGUARD ON DUTY sign. The adults murmured to each other over the wet heads of their children.

Inside the huddle, the Aryan mom, willowy and tanned (in *May*? Vain woman), was bent over Rory's small white body. His hair was mashed to his forehead. Brenna sat on the edge of the deep end, staring at her underwater feet.

More murmuring as Lily approached. She picked out "Where was she?" and "Wasn't even here this whole time," and "Looks like a grandmother." She had a vision of swinging her handbag like a scythe, cutting them all down like wheat. They didn't know anything. They had no idea.

"Let me through. Rory? Baby?" That sounded right, didn't it? "What happened to him?"

"Just got out too deep," someone said. "Got out over his head."

"His sister started screaming," someone else added.

The Aryan mom pressed, pressed, pressed on Rory's sternum, counting to herself. His lips were tinged with blue.

Lily knelt by the boy, getting the knees of her pantyhose wet. "Will he be all right?"

The male copy of the woman performing CPR looked down at Lily. He did not hide his opinion of her absenteeism. "Maybe."

The lioness was silent, slunk away into a cave or asleep in the heat of the sun. The huddle seethed and simmered like a cauldron of heretics.

Twin urges, at this moment: interrupt the woman's CPR and gather Rory into her arms, as if her embrace could cure all his ills; or get up calmly and run, run, run out of this hotel and out of Chicopee and out of Massachusetts. Run until her feet wore off. To Mexico, perhaps. Rory and Brenna would get sorted out; anyone who watched the evening news would see to that.

The blond woman breathed into Rory's mouth. Twice.

"We've gotta call 911," someone said.

"No," said Lily. They'd know about the Amber alert for sure. "No, wait a little longer. He might be okay."

The Aryan husband uttered a vocal exclamation point. "Are you nuts? He's got to get to a hospital. My wife can't do CPR forever."

"I already called," someone else said. "They're on their way."

Lily's blood froze. Rory coughed. Spluttered.

Breathing now. Opening his eyes. "Mommy?"

And then Brenna, at the other end of the pool room, in a howl that clanged from every reflective wall like the sword of the archangel: "*Where is my MOMMY?*"

When the ambulance screamed into the parking lot, Lily had her signal on, turning out, toward the Masspike. She was already making another to-do.

- Return van to Hertz
- Get home
- Hang pantyhose up to dry
- Make tea?
- Wait for the police

# Rich and Beautiful

I didn't work as an assistant concierge for very long; only two days. On the first day, I was mostly out in the city sweating through high-class errands—fresh pomegranates, artisan sodas, organic toothpaste. These desires were ridiculous to the girl still inside me, the girl from one of the lesser suburbs of St. Louis, the scrawny one who reassured herself daily that clean and neat was just as good as expensive and designer-branded.

But on the second day Donna sent me up to the eighteenth floor to help a family pack. They had been our guests for a week and were checking out in a hurry. She raised her eyebrows to herself as she gave me the room number. "Good luck," she murmured.

I stood there a moment longer. "Is there something I should know?"

The small muscles around her mouth tensed. "The Zariphes family are very good customers," she said. "Handle yourself well."

The room, 1809, was propped open with a wadded page from one of our complimentary magazines, and the interior was hardly recognizable. Debris was heaped on the king-size bed: a scattering of makeup-smeared tissues on one side, nothing on the other, and mounds of teenage-girl paraphernalia in the middle. Candy-colored lipsticks, nail polish and remover, paperbacks, an iPod in a pink rubber case, crumbling eyeshadow in dusted plastic boxes, last month's *Cosmopolitan,* and this week's *InTouch* were all disarranged in a column running down the center of the bed.

The rest of the room was also crowded with objects, and most of them were books. Stacks of paperbacks teetered against all available wall space. I could get the gist of the genres by running an eye over the colors and typefaces on the spines—lowercase white letters over swirling darkness, and lurid cursive embossed in red and orange. Vampire books, romance novels, and teen thrillers, a couple hundred of them. Suitcases stood here and there, and clothes lay on the floor, but mostly there were books. The room looked lived-in, long-term, by a sloppy librarian with terrible taste.

There were also two people in the room, a woman and a girl. The girl sat between the bed and the wall, a paperback in her hands. Her socked feet were propped up on the bedspread. The woman flitted from place to place, gathering clothes and stuffing them into a suitcase that lay open on the chrome baggage rack. She wore pearls and a silk blouse as finely wrought as a snowflake. I wasn't sure she had individual hairs growing out of her head so much as a series of satiny black curtains trimmed to perfection.

She caught sight of me. "Yes?"

"I'm here to help you pack," I said.

Her blank expression remained. I tried not to fidget and look at the floor, but the girl inside me found her accoutrements terrifying. "I'm from the concierge's office?"

"Oh. Yes." Throaty, intimate, a vague accent. She threw a hand at the girl sitting against the wall. "You can help Elodie."

The girl stirred, but did not lift her eyes from her book. She was about thirteen, not quite too young or too old for all the teenage flotsam in this room, and it was then I started actually wondering about the state of the room instead of just observing it. I sympathized with all the books, but *Cosmo* and the excess of makeup turned me off.

I went over to her and knelt. "Hey," I said. "Your name's Elodie?"

"It means white blossom," she said in a monotone, eyes on her book.

She didn't look much like a blossom, white or otherwise. She had olive skin and black hair that hung lank around her face. Her eyes were large, and her face was greasy and overpainted. She resembled the woman only as two blouses from the same factory, one paisley-patterned and one shell-colored, resemble each other. I was about to ask her if her book was any good when her mother snapped, "Get a move on, Elodie. We're leaving in one hour."

"Yeah, yeah," said the girl under her breath. She closed her book and lowered her feet to the carpet, looking at my chin instead of my eyes. "You're gonna help? The boxes are in there." She pointed at the closet.

I slid open one of the mirrored doors and found eight cardboard boxes, frayed with use. They'd been taped over many times, unfolded and reboxed. "I've got to get some tape from downstairs," I said.

Elodie reached under the bed, pulled out a tape-gun, and handed it to me.

I put the first box together, and Elodie piled books in it neatly. She did it in a particular order—half a stack here, half a stack there, three books from one pile, one book from another. It was a slow process, and I assembled two more boxes before she had filled the first. The woman went on floating around the room in her Louboutins until I heard a *clunk* behind me. I turned.

Elodie's mother gripped a perfume bottle, her wrist pressed into the dresser, the eau still sloshing. "Phillip and his attachments," the woman muttered under her breath, and left the room. Elodie watched her go, and shot a glance at me before turning back to her task.

"What's with all the books?" I said. I hoped rather than believed my tone was light.

She ignored the question. When she had filled the first box, and I was finished taping together the other seven, she said "You can do the rest of these," and bent to the column of girlthings on the bed.

I picked up a dozen paperbacks and placed them inside the second box, slapping the spines to straighten the pile. The books were worn at the edges, their bright colors flaking. "You've been here a week, right?"

"Yeah," said Elodie.

"This is kind of a lot of stuff to unpack for just a week, don't you think?"

She shrugged. "Nobody ever complained." There was a shadow of her mother in her face. "Until now."

Little brat. She plucked up from the bed, with the utmost care, used cotton balls from an apparent manicure. It occurred to me, finally, that 1809 had one king bed and there was no cot folded in the corner. Mother, father, and teenage daughter had to have slept in that one big bed.

My customer service gland released a directive. *Talk. Make a connection.* "How have you enjoyed staying in St. Louis?"

She shrugged again, saying nothing. I reminded my customer service gland that teenagers are immune to chitchat. She retrieved an L.L. Bean backpack from the bottom drawer of the dresser and plopped it on the bed. Smaller makeup sachets emerged from the backpack and Elodie distributed nail polish bottles, lipsticks, boxes of blush, and eyeliners among them.

I recognized one of her little zip-up bags as the same free gift I'd gotten at a Clinique counter last year. I'd been buying foundation for my mother, who loved nice things but didn't like spending money on herself. Jobs like this one, picked up at the beginning of a summer and laid down again a few thousand dollars later, made her ends meet as well as mine. Normally I scooped ice cream or spritzed perfume on sample cards at the mall. Guests at this hotel were not my crowd, but the hourly rate seemed too good to pass up just because the girl inside me was a little uncomfortable.

A man strode in through the open door. He frowned at me. "Who are you?"

"From the concierge—"

"Ah, yes," he said. He surveyed me, his eyes cool and transparent, like a wolf's. He had silver-streaked hair, and the gold jewelry on his wrists and fingers gave him an interesting two-toned look. His was plainly the clean side of the bed. He nodded at his daughter. "Elodie. Everything coming along?"

Elodie looked at the floor. "Yes, Daddy."

"Excellent," he said, and returned his attention to me. "Watch your hands. I don't want to find I'm missing anything when we land in New York." He strode out before what he'd said had a chance to sting.

"I'm sorry," said Elodie after a moment. Her voice had shed a layer of frost. "He's like that with everyone."

"I understand," I said. How dare he. I'd never so much as shoplifted lip gloss.

Elodie lowered her hands into her backpack. "I hate spending my whole summer this way," she said. "Every two weeks, pack, unpack, over and over. I hate it."

Apparently we were friends now. I pushed aside her father's words. "You usually stay two weeks in one place?"

She nodded.

"You only stayed a week in St. Louis."

She shrugged and zipped a makeup bag. "I dunno. Anyway, thanks. Not all the hotels have people like you. I have to do everything most of the time."

"Do you really unpack all these books every two weeks?" I asked.

She nodded again.

"Why?"

"They're my things," she said. "I look around and I see them, and I know they're mine. Even if nothing else in the room is."

"But it's a hotel room," I said, thinking of the little orientation speech Donna had given me the prior morning. Guests want a hotel room to be anonymous, she told me. They appreciate that they can come, abuse it briefly, and leave. The bed will be made up again for the next guest, the toilet paper folded into a new point. "It's not supposed to feel like home."

She was quiet. "Something has to," she said at last. Her eyeliner was crooked and too thick, overwhelming her green eyes. Either she was a poor student or her mother didn't bother to instruct her.

I taped the fifth box closed and started filling the sixth. The woman returned. "Has Phillip been in here?" she demanded, looking at her daughter. Elodie nodded. The woman took a step closer to me. "I want you to pack everything," she said. "I'll be back in twenty minutes, and I would like the room clear by then. Can you do that?"

She wasn't as imperious as her husband, but I still felt half my height as she spoke, as she met my eyes with her dark ones. I felt the cheap polyester of the hotel blazer brush my wrists, felt $4 shampoo fester on the dead protein of my hair. "Yes, ma'am."

"Thank you." She whiffed out again, leaving something floral behind. It reminded me of my mother's perfume: White Diamonds. No, it couldn't be. Too common.

"Her name is Adrienne," said Elodie. "That means rich and beautiful."

I said the only thing I could think of to keep the conversation going, which was "Does it suit her?" The answer was obvious, but Elodie's dissection of names had reminded me of my great-aunt Bess, who wouldn't let go of an introductory handshake until she decided whether the person's given name suited him or her. "You're too brunette to be a Cindy," Aunt Bess would declare, or "Harvey isn't nearly exciting enough. What about Jasper?" Her logic was generally beyond me, but I guessed she and this girl would have gotten along like gangbusters.

Elodie shrugged. "Everyone thinks she's rich and beautiful. Especially her."

"But what do you think?" I said. If she answered I was going to tell her about Aunt Bess. Maybe she'd smile about that. Maybe she'd look more like a blossom, instead of like a philodendron under office fluorescents, waxy and dull and growing sideways.

But she shrugged yet again. Maybe we weren't friends anymore.

I kept stacking books, eyeing the room more critically. Clothes hung in the closet, and foreign items were scattered across the sink in the bathroom. I'd have to repack the suitcase on the baggage rack. Everything in there was balled up and would wrinkle if left that way.

I filled the sixth box and checked my watch. "I think I need to pack your mother's things," I said. "Is there any way we can send the books along after you? I can pack the rest after you leave."

Her eyes widened under her mascara. "Leave without them?"

"They'd get sent to you. Today, probably. Your parents said you had to go soon."

"No," said Elodie. "I'm not leaving without them."

"All right," I said. I'd just have to hurry. I gathered the clothes on the floor and spread them on Phillip's side of the bed. I unwadded the clothes in the suitcase on the baggage rack and folded them neatly. I picked up the perfume bottle from the dresser. It was In Black by Estelle Ewen, a squat pink bottle with a black cap. I held it up for Elodie. "Does this go in with your makeup?"

She shook her head. "That's not mine."

"Is it your mother's?"

She shook her head again.

I left it on the dresser and zipped the suitcase. I found a Gucci train case in the bathroom and managed to fit all the counter's contents into it. (It was Quelques Fleurs, not White Diamonds. My nose told me that it had greater complexity, but the same effect: a bouquet rubbed against your gray matter like a mortar to a pestle.) The room started to bare up and look more like 1809, less like anyone's home.

I packed the hanging bag with Adrienne's rich and beautiful clothes and cleared the dirty tissues off her side of the bed. Elodie had thrown *Cosmo* and *InTouch* into the trash, but the books she dragged from city to city weren't much better.

I was taping up the last box when Phillip and Adrienne returned. Phillip leaned into the door frame, captivated by his BlackBerry. "Are you ready?" said Adrienne to her daughter. Elodie was yanking on the zipper of a small nylon suitcase, not nearly as nice as her mother's.

"Yes," she said, struggling.

I closed the suitcase for her. "I'll ring the bellboy to get all these," I said, gesturing at the boxes.

"Thank you," said Adrienne. "And thanks for your help with Elodie's things." Going by her tone, *Elodie's things* included reptiles and diseased rodents.

"It wasn't a problem," I said.

Adrienne retrieved her train case from the bathroom, walking right by the dresser and the bottle of perfume on top, as if it didn't exist. She put on a plum blazer that matched her skirt. She would be warm, but she looked the way she was supposed to look. "Come along," she said to her daughter. Elodie looked back at me and waved before the door shut on the three of them.

My shoulders relaxed. I looked at the dresser, and then I picked up the phone.

"We see them every year or so," said Donna, later, in her office. "No one knows what it is with them, why they're always traveling."

"Do they always get just the one king-size bed?"

There was a pause. "You noticed."

Adrenalin bloomed in my stomach. "A teenager sleeping with her parents? How could I not notice?"

Her glance was acidic. "We are paid not to notice what the guests do." She tamped down the edges of a few scribbled Post-Its stuck to the surface of her desk. "I hope they tipped you."

Some months later, no longer concerned about Donna, I Googled Phillip Zariphes. His picture was splashed all over society websites, he and Adrienne at galas galore, but his profession remained hidden behind pay walls. No press about him, nothing on LinkedIn. Finally, on an anonymous message board, I found the answer.

They were therapists, the pair of them, purveyors of a radical theory of relationships. They gave seminars every week of the year, balancing their business on word of mouth. Their central tenet was a cocktail of free love and strict anti-symbolism: you could do whatever you wanted to, whenever you wanted to, with whomever you wanted to, as long as you didn't gunk up your coupling with objects. No gifts, no fetish pieces, no money passing between lovers.

In that hour before my computer, I recalled that Adrienne had worn no exaggerated diamond on her third left finger. But Elodie's books were that much more mysterious. Pure sentiment—an attachment to objects that

Phillip and Adrienne wouldn't have withstood in a client. And as for the single king bed, I guessed that Relationship Open[ness], the brand and philosophy of their seminars, extended to daughters as well. I shuddered in my computer chair.

Here in Donna's office, I tapped the pocket of my polyester blazer, where I'd slipped the fat bottle of In Black after the bellboy trundled the last box out of the room. It would do for a tip from this family, whose money I didn't want, even not knowing what I came to know. I'd sniffed the cap: dark and sweet, like a kiss in an alleyway. Finding it, wherever Adrienne found it, must have been like reaching into her husband's pocket and pulling out a torn condom wrapper.

"Good," said Donna. She folded her hands.

I took a breath.

# Carlotta Made Flesh

A torn-up lotto scratcher blew about the brick walkway leading up to Charlotte's house. Jamie winced. Worse things had been strewn in front of this house, but Charlotte was particular about any kind of sloppiness out here, in front of the public.

GO RU, said one-half of the ticket. The LD SH half tumbled away toward the steep steps to the porch, which Charlotte had painted dark gray. After a brief chase, Jamie stuffed the halves of the scratcher into her purse and climbed the stairs and knocked. The porch still faintly stank of scrambled eggs. After an interval long enough that Jamie considered knocking again, Charlotte answered the door, as usual, in her bathrobe.

"Fuck," she said. "I was napping. Sorry."

Jamie closed the door. "Did you forget?"

"No way. I don't forget punctual people." She winked and sat down amid the rubbish on the couch: ad circulars, letters on creamy legal stationery, credit card bills, rolling papers. She picked up a roach and a purple Bic. "Want some?"

"Not today."

"Not today, not last week, not the week before." Charlotte sucked in a hit. "Why don't you ever get high with me?"

"I need my wits about me," said Jamie. "My keen journalistic nose."

"Pff." Charlotte dropped the lighter on the overflowing coffee table. "If your nose is so keen, what the fuck are you still doing here? You haven't gotten enough of me?"

"I just love buying you ice cream."

She sat up. "You bring me some?"

"I forgot."

She sat back. "Figures."

Jamie uncapped her pen. "Why don't you tell me about Estella?"

"Euuohhh, why do we have to talk about Estella?" Charlotte rubbed her hands over her short platinum hair. Her dark roots were so far beyond visible that the effect crossed over into a stylistic choice. "I'm through with Estella. She broke my heart."

Jamie'd switched on her digital recorder just in time to catch this. "Broke *your* heart."

"What do you call this?" Charlotte gestured at the dim living room. "The fucking…semi-life that I have now? I have the symptoms of major depression and the entire internet hates me. Or it's the other way around. Yeah, she broke my heart."

"A lot of people would say that *you* broke *their* hearts."

"There's journalist mode." Charlotte grinned. "You get this nasty smooth thing in your voice when you switch into journalist mode."

Jamie said nothing. Terry had counseled that you could get more from some subjects by clamming up than asking questions.

"Why don't I tell you about my childhood instead? Or some more about my marriage?"

Jamie twiddled her pen across her fingers, flipping it in neat ellipses while her other hand lay dormant. She'd taught herself to do it in high school. All the popular girls knew how.

"You know, you're like—it's like you got a book on your head. Level. Too level. Fucking *levelheaded*." Charlotte cackled and fell over into the papers scattered on the couch.

Half-baked already. "Why don't you clean all that up?"

"What, the couch?" Charlotte sighed and drew her robe together over her plump knees. "I don't know."

"Because your front porch, and the lawn—"

"That's different," said Charlotte. "That's outside. Anyone can see what's outside. No one comes in here."

"I do," said Jamie. "You do."

"You do, I do, we do, voodoo…"

"Estella," said Jamie. "Let's talk about Estella."

*

Estella was eleven years old, bright and bubbly, a lovely and well-behaved little girl. She had special affection for animals and yearned for a pet beagle. She liked knock-knock jokes and going to Girl Scouts and she thought up, on her own, an idea to raise more money for Troop #409, by selling coconut water in the summer along with the normal cornucopia of cookies. She enjoyed reading, but she liked funny movies better. She nagged her parents for trips to the zoo nearly every month and won a special ribbon at a school fair for her project on sloths.

But she kept coming home sick from Mrs. Potts' fifth-grade class. She missed out on several birthday parties because she felt too tired to go. Concerned about her weight loss and languor, her mom brought her to Dr. Margo, her pediatrician. A week later, Estella was told she had cancer. Leukemia.

She began a treatment regimen right away. She made up knock-knock jokes about her hair falling out and collected half a dozen new friends at her local clinic. She kept going to the zoo when she felt well enough. She faced the ordeal bravely, with more humor and optimism than anyone expected of such a young girl. Fortunately, her condition improved over time. After five months of treatment, the prognosis looked good, and she celebrated with a special cake shaped like a two-toed sloth.

There was just one problem with Estella.

*

"Yeah, her mom's a lunatic," said Terry.

"That's your opinion," said Jamie.

"It's anyone's opinion. It's the whole internet's opinion. Who am I to disagree with the whole internet?"

Sex had come first, and then, almost immediately after, Jamie reached for her laptop bag, which she'd slung ever so casually by the side of the bed while undressing. Since Terry was chummy with the features editor of *The Atlantic*, Jamie wanted to keep putting the Charlotte story in front of him as often as she put her tits in front of him. He could do a lot for her if Charlotte captured his attention. He knew she knew this, of course, and she knew he knew she knew. So they fucked first.

"The internet is a cauldron of sewage," she said.

"You sound like Jonathan Franzen."

"I'm just saying. You should disagree with the internet if you want to. You're disagreeing with shitty groupthink."

"I'd still think she was a lunatic even if it wasn't the internet's opinion," said Terry. He lit a cigarette and cracked his neck briskly. He was clad only in boxers and black socks. "Why are you doing this story, anyway?"

"You don't like it?"

"No, it's okay so far. Needs some dialogue, but the details are amazing. Did she really put all that out there? Knock-knock jokes about losing her hair?"

"Knock-knock," said Jamie.

"Who's there?"

"Bald eagles."

"Bald eagles who?"

"Bald eagles are the best kind of 'gles."

Terry stared.

"Girls? Baldy girls?"

He snorted. "That's stupid."

"She was *eleven*."

"No, she wasn't."

She sighed. "The point's the same. It's an eleven-year-old's kind of joke."

He got up and paced away from the bed. "Why are you doing this story, Jame?"

She shrugged and gazed at his cigarette, smoldering in the ashtray. Probably not a good idea to have a little jewel of heat sitting on the bedspread like that. "I can sell it," she said. "Nobody's done a long-form on Charlotte yet. Somebody ought to file something before her trials get going, before the AP makes her a du jour. It might as well be me."

"Nah," he said and leaned on the bed with both fists. The cigarette rolled toward her. "It's not just timing. There's a real reason for this story, this moment of your life. For long-forms there always is."

A few moments ticked by. Just a twitch of her head and Jamie could see a distorted, dark reflection of herself in the 60" flatscreen bolted to the wall. Her vague face in a black pool. "I guess I'd better go home," she said.

He sat on the bed, put his hands on her. "Says who?"

"I have more work to do."

"Kurt won't be home yet," said Terry, squeezing her breast.

She froze. "It doesn't matter," she said. "I work better without him around." She stubbed out Terry's cigarette and shut her laptop.

"Work here," he pleaded, following her out of the bedroom. "C'mon. I'll get you a glass of wine, you can put on some Schubert—"

"You just want to get laid."

He reached inside his boxers and wiggled his dick at her. "Maybe a little."

She zipped up her jeans.

Terry pushed his hands around her waist. "You do this to me." He crushed his face against her neck, her hair, intertwined his hand in hers and drew it down to his burgeoning hard-on. "Stick around a while."

*This is ridiculous*, Jamie thought, even as she went through the motions of kissing him back and helping him re-undress her. *You're a grown woman, a married woman, a know-better woman, and this is ridiculous.* Fucking on the floor, on her knees, in front of an arty mirror with table-saw blades collaged into a frame, Terry's breath hot on her ear while he pounded at her. *This is ridiculous.* She was still thinking it getting into her car an hour later, still thinking it trying to find the right ramp for the 405 northbound. They were doing construction, interminably, between the 10 and the Sepulveda Pass, and some of the northbound exits closed after 10 PM. Jamie could never keep straight which ones, but now they practically all seemed to be closed. She drove in circles, following one DETOUR sign and then another, finally going southbound to Pico and getting off and making a U and going back north. It was six fruitless highway miles, and she lost half an hour trying to find her way.

*This is ridiculous.*

Kurt was not at their apartment in Toluca Lake when she finally got there. His transitioning from day shift to second shift to occasional night shifts had been so gradual that she'd been putting up with it for many months before realizing it was something to put up with. Operating room nurses did well, better than struggling freelancers (which was merely a nice face on *failed writer*, given that she hadn't actually freelanced anything for money since quitting her public relations job eighteen months earlier), but her husband was starting to feel like a stranger, like a smooth-tempered clinical-smelling roommate. This slow unknitting between them, loop by loop, didn't feel worth any amount of salary.

She listened to the empty apartment. Kurt's absence didn't explain or excuse Terry, of course. Nothing did.

*This is ridiculous.*

*

Charlotte Santangelo had a very ordinary life up until her 37th year. She grew up in Los Angeles, went to Cal State Long Beach, worked as a paralegal, took vacations to Catalina and Hawaii. At 25 she married Barrett McAvoy, a 28-year-old financial adviser she met at a downtown club. She kept her maiden name—not for any political reason, but just because she liked it rolling off her tongue better than McAvoy. Soon, the pair bought a house not quite inside Bel Air and, by all appearances, made ready to start a family. Charlotte told friends that she couldn't wait to have kids, especially a daughter. She laughed about how she and Barrett ceremoniously cast her birth control pills into the fire pit on their patio.

Years of increasingly desperate measures to conceive followed. Although both husband and wife had mild fertility issues—Charlotte didn't ovulate with regularity, Barrett's sperm count was low—their chances were good. Wanting to avoid multiple births, doctors continually warned them away from expensive, invasive procedures, counseling them to just keep trying.

When interviewed, Charlotte can't provide a consistent answer as to why the couple did not adopt. She says she was dubious about loving someone else's child, and then she says Barrett refused even though she begged him. She says foreign adoption was out of the question but won't say why. It is another aspect of her story, like so many, that is too slippery for an observer to understand completely.

Soon after Charlotte turned 32, they gave up trying. She had stopped working in preparation for motherhood, and she chose not to find another job. Barrett was doing well enough to support them easily. She volunteered at animal shelters and museums. She even spent a few months as a sort of candy striper in an oncology ward at Children's Hospital Los Angeles, but found that work too difficult for a longer engagement. For a year, and then two years, and then three, Charlotte drifted.

*

I WANT MY MONEY BACK BITCH.

Jamie had brought ice cream this time, and a good thing, too, because someone had spray-painted these six words on the gray boards of Charlotte's porch. She couldn't miss them, even if she only answered the door and didn't actually step outside. Jamie walked around to the screened sun porch at the back of the house. The porch door was unlatched, but the French doors into the house were locked (and black-curtained). She knocked.

"Who's there?"

"It's Jamie."

Charlotte was dressed, but disheveled, in stained yoga pants and a rumpled t-shirt. "Why aren't you at the front door?"

"It doesn't matter. I brought you some Cherry Garcia."

Charlotte took the pint and stood there silent.

"Come on, let's go in."

"What happened to the porch?"

"Let's just go in and—"

"*What happened to the porch.*" She bolted to the front of the house and yanked open the door. Jamie followed. Charlotte's shoulders fell. "Goddammit."

"C'mon," said Jamie, closing the door and leading her into the living room by tugging on the ice cream in her hand. "Let's get a spoon."

"Estella loved ice cream," Charlotte mumbled. She curled up on her sofa around the pint's cold core. "She liked Rocky Road, though. Not Ben & Jerry's. I think only grownups like Ben & Jerry's."

She nattered on under her breath while Jamie rummaged for a spoon in the kitchen. It smelled dank and overripe in there, a kind of higher-volume version of the smell in the rest of the house. Like a greenhouse watered too vigorously and left to rot.

None of the silverware was clean. Packages of flowered paper plates and red Solo cups stood open on the counters. Flimsy boxes of cutlery were overturned and empty. She found a handful of plastic spoons in a drawer and returned to the living room. Charlotte was still talking, babbling for some reason about the books she read as a teenager.

Jamie tapped her with the spoon and she sat up. "And I liked mythology. Edith Hamilton. Whole generations of kids have read that book. You know about Sisyphus?" She spooned up a hunk of ice cream and licked at it. "The guy who rolled the rock up the hill over and over? That's how I feel about this house. Like a fuckin...like a job that never ever gets done. Like doing the dishes. You're washing the same fuckin dishes every day, you know. You never do get 'em clean." She stabbed at the ice cream.

"Yes, you do," said Jamie. Matter-of-factness could maybe head off the squall she foresaw. "You get them clean every time. It's maintenance. Not a one-time thing."

Charlotte threw the spoon into a corner, put the ice cream on the table and dropped into the couch face-first. "FUCK YOU," she shouted at the cushion. "FUCK YOU, ZEUS. I'VE BEEN PUNISHED ENOUGH."

"That's what I think too," Jamie said quickly. "That's just what I think, Charlotte, that you've been punished enough. I want to get that message out to people, but you've got to help me, okay? You've got to stop throwing tantrums like this and cooperate with me."

"Cooperate." A dry husk of a chuckle. "Cooperate with you. You sound like a PR lackey from the Third Reich. Go away, Jamie. I don't want to talk to you today."

"But—"

"GO AWAY!" she shrieked.

Jamie waited, but Charlotte wheezed into the sofa, subpoenas fluttering around her, for several minutes. Jamie got up and put the ice cream in the freezer, which also held an empty bottle of vodka and a box of Stouffer's family-size macaroni and cheese. She left the house as quietly as possible.

Using her phone, she found the closest Home Depot and drove there and bought spray-paint remover, sponges, gloves, sandpaper, and paint trays. She let herself into the sun porch and retrieved a can of the gray paint left over from when Charlotte redid the porch. Night fell during the hour it took her to sand off and paint over the ghost of I WANT MY MONEY BACK BITCH, but she felt parlessly virtuous when finished. She drove over to Terry's house, fucked him for twenty-five minutes, and shut herself in his bathroom with her laptop.

*

Estella got better, but then she relapsed. She improved, and then relapsed again. As soon as word spread of her condition, a cast of dozens stepped forward to help. The local effort was heart-melting—families volunteering to drive, cook, clean, and lend any amount of other help to the stricken girl and her parents.

Soon, Estella's story grew beyond her small Midwestern town. She was a prolific poster in forums related to animals and made a lot of friends across the country through online gaming on her PC and her Xbox. Messages and offers of help poured in from all these acquaintances, most of whom followed her mother's blog for news about her. Her story spread as stories on the internet do, from hand to hand, link to link, post to post.

Before long, the question of money arose. Estella's mom was a teacher, and her circle of online friends concluded that this meant she couldn't afford Estella's cancer treatments. Kind souls across the world asked to be allowed to donate to her medical fund. Estella refused, and requested that her "lovelies" instead buy Girl Scout cookies or contribute to the World Wildlife Fund. Such selflessness meant that her legend, and the affection directed toward her, only grew.

All this time, residents of the small Wisconsin town where Estella and her mother lived were growing

*

Knock knock knock. "Jamie, I have to *pee*."

"Go in the sink," she called.

"I'm not a fucking animal. Open up."

"I'm working," she called, a little louder.

BANG. "Open the goddamn door."

She snapped the computer closed and got up, grumbling, to let Terry in. He shoved her out and slammed the door. "Hey-y," she protested. "That hurt."

"Go write in your own bathroom."

The same exits, from Sunset south, were closed again, and Jamie looped in the same stupid circles, following the same deceptive DETOUR signs, until she lost her patience and went south on the freeway. This time, she decided to try taking Santa Monica Boulevard all the way northwest to the 101, one of the least intelligent decisions she'd made all week. It took her nearly an hour to get home.

On the drive, the ill-used muscles from her porch mission stiffened up. She winced getting out of the car. A glass of Merlot was foremost in her mind.

Kurt was home, sipping a Fat Tire, his skin ultra-dark in his teal nurse's scrubs. His sterile OR smell filled the kitchen. "Hey, honey," he said, and got up to kiss the corner of her mouth. "Bad day?"

"Charlotte wouldn't talk to me. Someone spray-painted her porch again." She got down a wineglass and filled it over halfway.

He tsked. "Too bad."

"What about you?"

"Twenty-two-year-old with a freaky uterine tumor. It was playing havoc with her moods, boy." He half-laughed. "Her roommates didn't know what the heck to do with her."

Jamie gulped wine. "I'll bet."

"Have you had dinner?"

"I'm not…nothing sounds good to me."

"Mind if I have the rest of the chili?"

She gestured and had another swallow of wine. "Knock yourself out. I'm gonna work for a while."

She'd unloaded her things and started into the study with her laptop when Kurt said, "If she wouldn't talk to you, why're you home so late?"

A flashbulb popped in her brain, whiting out her vision. "The, um. The traffic."

He leaned against the doorway and sipped his beer. "Traffic? This time of day?"

"Yeah. The 405 exits on the Westside are all closed. I took Sunse—um, Santa Monica. Took me forever."

He shrugged a little. "Yeah, but still. It's after midnight, Jamie. Where you been?"

"I went to see Terry," she said. The key to the Big Lie: mix falsehood with fact. "Asked him about the story. We went over it for a while."

"Oh, Terry," said Kurt, loose-limbed again. "How's he doing?"

"He's fine," said Jamie. She was perspiring. "Just had a piece in the *Times* magazine."

Kurt looked reluctantly impressed. "Good for him." He pointed into the kitchen with his beer hand. "You work. Imma eat me some chili."

Jamie smiled him out into the hall, locked her study door, and leaned against it. Her wedding ring burned. *This is ridiculous.*

*

Eventually, Charlotte found a new hobby: the internet. She started with Bejeweled, Scrabble, and other online casual games. Then she began following a wide array of message boards, well over a dozen, focusing on subjects from Greek mythology to quilting. She had always nurtured a colorful spectrum of interests, and the limitless possibilities of internet pursuits meshed well—or, perhaps, fatally—with her personality.

Over the following two years of immersion in online games, online conversations, online friendships, Charlotte's connections to the outside world became ever thinner and more tenuous. She quit her volunteer jobs. She stopped going with her husband to business functions, and then she stopped going with him to friendly dinners, and then she stopped going with him on vacations. She gained weight. She began having her groceries delivered and bought a $2,000 custom computer chair so she could sit comfortably for long periods. Although she kept up with the gardening and maintenance necessary to keep the outside of her house beautiful, the inside was a shambles.

Barrett had no idea what had happened to the beautiful, vivacious woman he married. They visited a couples counselor for a few months, to little result. The year she turned 36, he filed for divorce. Despite her age, the court found Charlotte unsuitable for employment and awarded her generous alimony. Barrett's checks allowed her to live essentially the same lifestyle as before. So, she tumbled deeper, and deeper still, into the rabbithole of internet-only contact with the outside world.

At some point, she began assuming multiple names online. She is not clear on when this practice began, and the records of her online life, voluminous yet incomplete, resist ordinary research. But after Barrett moved out, Charlotte began posting more and more under an identity she had created as a kind of bright mirror to her own: Carlotta, a Midwestern teacher and mother of one.

Carlotta became all the motherly, optimistic models of life that Charlotte couldn't be. She was cheerful and Christian and endlessly empathetic. She made dozens of friends through groups related to casual games and amateur landscape painting, through Facebook and Pinterest, and through the blog she kept about her life, Surviving Happy. One of the most popular subjects on this blog was her eleven-year-old daughter, Estella.

*

"Look at this," said Charlotte, and held her spread hands up to the weak light filtering in the half-open blinds. "Look at my fingers."

"What about your fingers?"

"*Look*. At the manicure. See?"

She had light blue polish on her nails. "Pretty color," said Jamie.

"Through the light, goddammit. Don't you notice anything?"

"Um…"

Charlotte dropped her hands to her lap with an exasperated noise and immediately held them up again. "Look at the way the light shines through my nails," she said. "You can see every brushstroke. I did these myself. Every little mistake, where the polish is too thick or too thin. It looks fine any other way, like this—" she brought her hands down and played her fingers across her robed knees "—but up against the light like this, all you can see is flaws."

Jamie looked. The thick shadows of the polish on her fingernails showed striations, like wood grain. And patched crescents were visible where Charlotte had wiped away the edges of her work and painted over them. Her pinky nails were twice as long as any of the other eight. "But no one ever sees your manicure like that," Jamie said. "They only see it from the top, and it looks fine."

"No one ever sees my manicure, period," said Charlotte, and hid her hands in the cuffs of her robe. "Except you."

"I keep coming here," said Jamie, attempting to smile. "I want to get your story told."

"You want to get my story *published*. Let's not fuck around, here."

"Right. Published. Show the world you're not a monster."

"And show the world you're not a third-rate journalist."

Jamie said nothing. Charlotte picked up a ridiculous glass bong with purple marbling and protrusions shaped like leaves and mushrooms and bubbled up a hit. She offered the smoking thing to Jamie, who shivered her head no.

"Oh, come on," said Charlotte. "Fucking relax. I'm just trying to put everyone's cards on the table."

"Then put yours out, too," said Jamie. "Why'd you pretend to be Estella?"

"*Why?*" Charlotte crawled off the couch and staggered for the kitchen, laughing. "*Why?* Because I was *lonely*. And delusional. And greedy. Didn't you know that?" She returned with a box of Wheat Thins, slouched back down, ate a few.

Jamie wrote something in her Moleskine and recrossed her legs.

Charlotte watched her for a moment. "You know, I'm not a loser," she said.

Uh. "I don't think you are."

"Pu-leeze. Yes, you do. And I understand it looks that way. I may have fucked my life up, but I'm not actually stupid. I see most things." She drew her first two fingers in a V across her face, first right hand, then left: the Batusi. "I see what my life looks like from the outside: fat, divorced, pushing forty, living for the internet." She inhaled, exhaled. "And I see my own disgrace. It's something I accept."

"But it's not like that," Jamie began to say.

"I mean, I might not have a good marriage, or a nice car, or a talent for writing. Like you. But I'm not a loser. That's not how I want you to think of me." She got up for the kitchen again.

"Charlotte, I swear, I don't think of you like that," Jamie called in. She was perspiring again, her face hot-cold.

Water hissed briefly in the kitchen sink and Charlotte came back carrying a red Solo cup. "I still have some control over what people see when they…" Something caught her eye out the front window. "What the—*fuck*—" She dropped her cup and bolted to the door.

"Hey, hold on—" Jamie got up and snatched at Charlotte's arm—she was nothing like presentable to the outside world—but she charged onto the porch, barefoot, her body joggling under her slip.

A few feet away on the lawn, near the blond sidewalk, an older man in a UCLA hat and a generously sized aloha shirt crouched next to a golden retriever. Both creatures were evacuating their bowels.

"What are you *doing*?" screamed Charlotte.

The man flipped her the bird. "Go fuck your fake daughter."

"You *animal*. You fucking *monster*. I'm gonna *tear* your goddamn *face* off!"

Jamie caught Charlotte and held her bodily, smelling the rank robe, her left ear gradually going numb from the commotion. Charlotte flung her arms wildly toward the spectacle on the lawn and descended into bellowing various iterations of "Fuck!" over and over. She was not a strong woman, though, her big body lax from years of computerist sitting, and Jamie managed to drag her inside even before the aloha-shirted man had pulled up his cargo shorts.

*

Eventually, Estella relented, and her mother helped her open a PayPal account for donor contributions. She kept a counter available to show how much had been given. The fund grew, at first rapidly and then steadily. In three months, it had over $550,000 from some 75,000 donors. Estella's story had been passed from screen to screen all over the world, and everyone who heard of her was eager to help.

Six months after the fund opened, doubts surfaced. Persistent commenters on news stories and blog posts about Estella pointed out medical inconsistencies with her story. The pattern of her recovery and relapse did not cohere with her diagnosis, experts said. And people from Estella's hometown in Wisconsin began to come forward, saying they'd never heard of her or her mother.

A Gawker reporter interviewed the principal of Estella's school. No record of her existed. An anonymous Vital Records worker in Wisconsin leaked that no birth certificate could be found with her name or her mother's. An enterprising Redditor discovered that the IP address from which Estella posted content wasn't in Wisconsin, but California.

When these questions were brought to her website and Facebook page, Estella reacted with hurt feelings and asked for patience and understanding. "I know you have a lot of questions about my story," she wrote, "and I promise I'll answer them. Have faith in me just a little longer." She signed the note with her trademark "Estell★."

The following morning, all trace of her had vanished from the internet. Her website was gone, her fundraising site was gone, her Facebook account and page had been deleted. It was as if she'd never existed.

*

"Stop it," said Jamie. Terry was fucking her from behind (again) and from time to time he gave her rear end a ringing slap. She hated it, and anyway she worried it would leave a mark that Kurt would see.

Slap.

"*Stop* it."

"Just a little more."

She looked at the clock by the bed. 9:54. The exit ramps would close at ten.

Slap.

"Goddammit, Terry." She yanked away from him and stood up.

He overbalanced, fell, and shouted into the rumpled duvet. "What the *fuck*?"

"I told you to stop," she said, and snatched her underwear from the carpet.

He turned over and fixed her with a black glare. "You bitch," he said. He began jerking off. "You *bitch*. Unh. *Bitch*."

Grabbing up her clothes, Jamie fled to the living room.

She got stuck on Wilshire and didn't make it to the 405 in time. The car in front of her for fifteen minutes of brake, crawl, brake, crawl was a late-90s Mustang with a custom license plate frame. LIFE IS A TREASURE, it read. It was decorated with small colored cabochons. Five of the eight stones were missing.

She couldn't stop thinking about the scene at Charlotte's. That perfectly normal-looking man, befouling her lawn. And Charlotte, screeching. The heat and weight of her body such a shock.

The pattern of Wednesdays at Charlotte's (and at Terry's) was so ingrained, the work of breaking apart and reassembling Charlotte/Carlotta[/Estella] so much a *job*, that Jamie had forgotten the body and brain behind the life she was trying to sanctify. She could smell Charlotte when she sat across from her; she could see the evidence of her eating and smoking weed, and she could hear her voice; but Charlotte hadn't been a physical human, with a beating heart beneath her breasts, until she'd been in Jamie's arms. Prior to that, she'd been a kind of digital entity with a human face, a creature birthed of zeroes and ones. More a Carlotta made flesh than a Charlotte, grown at one time from girl to woman and sentient in every hour of that life, only latterly entubated and made effigy.

Losing patience with the Wilshire exit, Jamie U-turned away from LIFE IS A TREASURE and headed for Santa Monica Boulevard. Both ramps were closed there, north and south; on to Pico, where both were closed, too. She pulled into a dark, leafy side street, yanked on the brake, and rested her forehead on the steering wheel. Heat pressed into her sternum. Her labia stung from Terry's lust. "I just want to go home," she said into her car.

*

A week after Surviving Happy vanished, along with everything else about Estella, the Huffington Post broke the news that the whole story—the mother, the daughter, the cancer, the sites, everything—had been fabricated by one woman, a divorced 37-year-old Los Angeles resident named Charlotte Santangelo.

The internet summarily called for her head. Those taken in by her wanted her arrested, sued, lynched, skinned alive. Financial supporters wanted their money back, but something far more complex, something not returnable, was also at stake for these people. They'd trusted Estella, they'd given their hearts and prayers to her. They couldn't have their hearts back, so they wanted to tear out Charlotte's and feast upon it.

Charlotte had no defense. She gave a terrible, unflattering interview to The Daily Beast and released a confused statement to the press that generally made everyone madder. It sounded as if she didn't regret her actions. She seemed to feel that all the publicity related to Carlotta and Estella was about *her*, not about those who were duped by her. Pop psychologists opined that she was ill, that she deserved pity rather than censure.

*

On Tuesday Charlotte texted to ask if Jamie could come later, around nine, the next day. Jamie texted back in the affirmative. But this was the final Wednesday, she'd decided. All Charlotte wanted to do was sit around in a dark sweatsock of a house, getting high and occasionally getting irrational in tears or tantrums. Jamie could write the rest of the story without her. It might've helped to hear Charlotte's actual views on the whole debacle, but apparently that turnip had no blood.

She decided to go to Terry's first, and to give herself only half an hour there. Enough time for him to read the latest and give her his opinion, but not enough time for him to fuck her.

*For me to fuck him,* she corrected herself. *I'm the one fucking him. I'm fucking him to get into* The Atlantic. *It's not him fucking me.*

She made a mental note to stop by Vendome on the way home from Charlotte's and pick up some of that small-batch beer Kurt liked. Pliny the Elder. She'd missed Kurt, his agreeable nature and his humble opinion of himself, across all these Wednesdays. And she'd taken to humming or shaking her hair out of her face whenever the Kurt in her mind asked the question she hoped the real Kurt never knew enough to form, the question that felt like little more than a dumb repeated vowel: why, why, why.

Twilight had vanished by the time she merged onto the 405. In the darkness, a swath of light cut curving into the mountain over the Sepulveda Pass. The tail of red stretching south, away from Jamie, was overwhelmed by the lazy white lasso of headlights winding north, toward her. *It looks like a river,* she thought. *A river of light.*

*

Today, four months after the implosion, Charlotte deserves pity more than ever. Not just because she is a pitiable woman. Not just because she will receive censure enough from the courts when they finally organize all the suits and charges against her. Not just because she couldn't track down and return all of the $1.2 million in mostly anonymous donations to Estella's fund if she spent the rest of her life trying, nor because she hasn't spent a dime of that money on herself. She deserves the internet's forgiveness not only because of what she is, but because of what the internet is.

It's a miracle, a wonder of the world. It's a place of such versatile and inexhaustible fertility that anything can flourish there—art, ideas, fraud, wealth, work, play, pornography, evil, communion, truth. Charlotte was one of its most well-versed citizens, someone who knew better than most what she was getting into when she created Carlotta and Estella (and Charmaine and Felix and Lettie and half a dozen other identities). She feels remorse, but she should not. Loneliness produced her behavior, but so did her primary environment. After all, she only took donations for Estella when too many people insisted on it for her to keep turning them down.

*

"You're proselytizing," said Terry. "Big-time."

"So what?"

"So you're supposed to *report*, not insist on a point of view," said Terry. "This is seriously biased. Back off and let people draw their own conclusions."

"I'm drawing conclusions on purpose," said Jamie. "I'm trying to write about the internet. This is important to me."

"Then write a fucking blog. Long-forms can make points, but you're giving a sermon."

Jamie actually drew her tongue between her front teeth and bit down on it.

"And the conclusion's even worse." He lit a cigarette and got up to pace. "The way you built it up is good, switching between the two of them so it's not obvious how they're related. It makes for a good story, especially for people who might not've heard of her. But this last part is ridiculous, Jame." He smoked and looked at her. "It's like you're trying to save her soul."

"What if I am?" said Jamie.

"*The Atlantic* doesn't give a fuck about that. Or her. And neither should you."

She closed the laptop and stood up. "I gotta go."

*

Of course, Charlotte didn't have to lie in the first place. She didn't have to create Estella's cancer or perpetuate it. But it was a story she was telling to herself, at first, and then to just a handful of others. Like all imaginative storytellers, Charlotte had to go where the tale took her.

Estella inspired tens of thousands of people without even existing. What separates her from Jane Eyre but context?

Charlotte Santangelo does not deserve to live in shame. She is a lonely, imaginative woman who channeled her energy in the wrong direction. She could be any of us. She could be anyone who has found herself in water too deep and dark to float upon.

*

The dogshit and humanshit were still on the lawn. Someone had slashed CUNT in black paint—not spray-paint, *paint*—on the front walk. The door stood ajar, the porch light on.

"Carlotta?" Why had she said that? *Charlotte.* "Are you in there?" She pushed open the door. The house was completely dark. Jamie crept in, felt silly, took a big step, fell heavily over something lying on the foyer rug.

She had no idea where the light switches were, how to get to the lamps. She fumbled in her purse for the LED flashlight she kept on her keychain.

It was Charlotte, the thing she'd tripped over, lying face-down. She wore only panties and her hands were stained a tired red.

"Oh, shit." With effort, Jamie turned her over. Charlotte's body was warm, and she mumbled and moved her head at Jamie's touch.

Three long slashes, inflamed and oozing slow blood, marked each of her cheeks.

"Oh *fuck*. Charlotte. Charlotte, wake up." She shook her arms, patted the back of her left hand like a grandmother.

"Wake up. Who did this? Who did this to you?" Jamie got out her phone, smeared blood on the screen unlocking it, felt her stomach heave. "Charlotte!" She tried dialing 911 but the phone was confused by the blood. "Charlotte, wake up."

"Nnn. Don't—don't—"

"Oh thank God. Charlotte, who did this? I'm calling an ambulance."

"Noooo…" She trailed off into a groan. "Don't call… anyone. 'Mallright. Leeme lone."

"You're bleeding all over."

"Too late f'me. Doneed."

"It's *not* too late, Charlotte! I'm calling an ambulance."

"Stop." Charlotte put a bloody hand over Jamie's phone. "They gimme surjry. Fix it pretty. Donwanna be. Better thisway."

She kept half-rising on an elbow and slipping, thocking her head on the floor. The cuts on her face were crooked and terrible. They didn't look fresh, but they didn't look too well-clotted, either. Something awful was rising up in Jamie's mind. Charlotte finally got her eyes all the way open and chuckled faintly at her. "'Mnot a ghost," she said. "'Mnot dying." She sighed. "Been here all day. Gimme some water."

She lolled off again on the floor. After a moment, Jamie put her phone down and used her tiny flashlight to get to the kitchen, leaving Charlotte in the dark. Cockroaches scuttled in the sink when the light swept them. Jamie drew two Solo cups of water and went back to the foyer. On the way she passed a lamp and switched it on, and Charlotte groaned. Jamie helped her sit up, trying to avoid accidentally touching her breasts or grabbing handfuls of her fleshy body. She tipped the Solo cup gently against Charlotte's mouth.

"Mm. 'Sbetter."

"What happened?"

"Took too many," said Charlotte. "Valium. Dint wanna die. Jus sleep all day. Not see m'face."

"You took them this morning?" Slow nod. Too late for a stomach pump, then. She'd live or die on what was already in her bloodstream. "Who did this to your face?"

"Me."

The something awful thunked down in Jamie's gut. "You did it to your*self*?"

Charlotte nodded down into the Solo cup.

Jamie took a deep breath. She thought back to what she'd seen in movies about overdoses. "You need some coffee."

"Mebbe." Charlotte reached up to her face and winced.

"Please let me take you to the hospital."

"Threw eggs at me lassnight. Rang the door n when I came, egg egg egg." She laughed, a big weird sound from a slumped, still body. "My robe's a mess. Tookt off."

"Why did you do this, Charlotte. Why." Jamie was crying.

"'M the pariah." She grinned, which opened up the edges of two of her wounds in a hideous way. "Might 'swell look the part."

"But my article," said Jamie. "It was going to fix things. I said…I said you didn't deserve shame."

Charlotte looked at her as if she'd lost her mind, kind of dopily. "Course I do," she said. "Fuckin…course I do. 'Snothing else I deserve. Shame n shame n shame." She picked up the other Solo cup and tossed its contents in her face. The water and blood dripped down, staining her breasts, and she grinned on and on, serenely.

*Wire Mothers*

# Acknowledgments

Grateful acknowledgment is made to the following publications, in which these stories appeared in slightly different form:

"Between 4 and 6" in *Rhythm & Bones*, July 2019.
"The First Snow" in *Storm Cellar*, February 2018.
"To-Do" in *The Doctor T.J. Eckleburg Review*, January 2015.

My gratitude to:

Miette. Everyone at Whisk(e)y Tit.

Cathy Ulrich. Debra di Blasi. Amber Sparks. Tommy Dean.

Matt, as ever, as always. I should've dedicated this one to you, but you were blessed with a cloth mother.

# About the Author

Katharine Coldiron is the author of *Ceremonials*, a novella, and *Junk Film*, a collection of criticism. Find her at kcoldiron.com or on social media @ferrifrigida.

# About the Publisher

**WHISKEY TIT** attempts to restore degradation and degeneracy to the literary arts. We are unwilling to sacrifice intellectual rigor, unrelenting playfulness, and visual beauty, putting forth texts that would otherwise be abandoned in a homogenized literary landscape.

In a world gone mad, our refusal to make this sacrifice is an act of civil service and civil disobedience alike, and our work reflects this. We welcome like-minded readers and writers.

www.ingramcontent.com/pod-product-compliance
Lightning Source LLC
Chambersburg PA
CBHW071951190726
48293CB00004B/1426